DOCTOR MENACE!

BEANObooks

published under licence
meadowside
CHILDREN'S BOO

NIT NURSE

The kids of Beanotown School were in the grip of terror. The headmaster had locked all the doors and windows. He had stationed teachers to guard all possible escape routes. Class by class, the pupils were lining up in the corridor outside the sick bay, their knees knocking and their palms sweaty.

It was time for the yearly visit from the nit nurse.

"I'm gonna run in circles so fast that she'll get too dizzy to see straight," said Billy.

"You did that last year," said Curly.
"I saw her arriving with a huge net –
you're done for, mate!"

Billy started to pace up and down,
gnashing his teeth.

"I'm gonna squirt that anti-nit
shampoo of hers right in her face,"
said Minnie with a fierce scowl.
"Then I'll run for it before she can
catch me."

"She's on to that
wheeze too," Pie
Face told her in
a panic.

SICK
BAY

"She's wearing goggles this year."

"That low-down, dirty trickster!" snarled Minnie.

Suddenly the sick bay door flew open and Fatty Fudge waddled out, clutching his arm and groaning. A hand shot out of the room, clutched Billy by the collar and dragged him

in, slamming the door behind him.

For a moment they heard the sound of running footsteps. Then there was a loud WHUMP sound, just like someone being rugby-tackled to the floor. Minnie, who was next in line, started to bite her nails.

"Is your head bleeding?" Curly asked Fatty Fudge. "That nit nurse uses her comb like she's trying to scalp you!"

"Never mind my scalp," sniffed Fatty. "This year she's giving us injections as well!"

A gasp of horror went up from the waiting kids, and there was a loud thump as Walter the Softy fainted for the eighth time that morning. Then a head of black, scruffy hair rose above the crowd.

"You pack of softies might be giving in, but that nitty old nurse isn't getting hold of the Menace's hair!" Dennis declared. "She's never managed it yet, and she's not gonna start this year."

"Gnash!" agreed Gnasher.

"Menaces like us don't get nits anyway," Dennis went on.

"If you haven't got nits, then there isn't any harm in letting her check for them, is there?" said Bertie Blenkinsop in his most pompous voice.

Dennis narrowed his eyes and leaned towards Bertie until their noses were almost touching.

Bertie gulped.

"Trouble is, fish face, she might come across some of Gnasher's super-menacing fleas while she's checking," Dennis explained.

"Fleas?" squealed Bertie. "Ugh, get away from me, you dirty menace!

I bet you have got nits!"

"Not likely," said Dennis with a wide grin. "Didn't you know that nits like clean hair? They wouldn't wanna live on my head when there's a sweet-smelling softy one like yours around!"

"Mummy!" wailed Bertie, clutching his hair in horror.

Dennis shook his head and turned to Curly and Pie Face.

"There's no way she's getting hold of Gnasher's fleas," he said. "And as for injections, she's not sticking any needles into me!"

"But you never get colds anyway," said Curly.

"Yeah, I'm too strong for them, but I can still catch the stinking-cold viruses and pass them on," Dennis explained. "The best menace of winter is giving softies the sniffles!"

The door opened again and Billy zoomed out so fast that all they saw was a blur.

He shot through the locked doors at the end of the corridor, leaving a Billy-shaped hole there. Minnie started to shriek, but the burly arm of the nit nurse dragged her in and slammed the door.

"You lot can stand here if you want, but I'm gonna find a way out!" Dennis declared. "Come on, Gnasher!"

Dennis raced down the corridor and climbed through the hole Billy had made. Now there was just one more set of doors between him and freedom! Just then he heard footsteps hurrying towards him. It was the headmaster and Mr Pump. Dennis ducked around

the corner, pressed himself against the wall and held his breath. Gnasher did the same.

"I see Billy has made his escape," said the headmaster. "Stand here, Mr Pump, and stop any more of the little horrors . . . er . . . I mean the dear little children trying to get out."

"Yes sir!" bawled Mr Pump, saluting the headmaster.

"Above all," the headmaster hissed, "keep Dennis in there. The nit nurse has surpassed herself this year. She has created a special machine called the Dennis Device. It will hold him still while she checks his hair and injects him. If this machine works, we will make one for all Dennis's teachers! I am sure that his parents would like one as well!"

"It sounds incredible!" Mr Pump gasped.

"All she has to do is get him into the room and the machine will do the rest," said the headmaster. "It was made by Professor Nutjob himself."

"But how will she get Dennis into the machine?" asked Mr Pump.

Dennis and Gnasher craned forward to listen.

"She won't need to," laughed the headmaster. "Dennis will be unable to resist."

The headmaster whispered into Mr Pump's ear, and the PE teacher burst into laughter.

"A stroke of genius!" he chortled. "Dennis is doomed! His days of menacing are numbered!"

The headmaster strode off down the corridor and Dennis stared at Gnasher in horror.

"A Dennis Device?" he whispered. "We can't let her test that out! I'll never be able to menace again!"

"GNASH!" said Gnasher, biting his lip.

What if she had created a Gnasher Device as well?

Mr Pump was now standing between Dennis and the exit, so he had to find another way out – and fast! It was only a matter of time before the nit nurse realised he had left the queue. He sped along the corridor, checking each window as he went, but they were all locked and bolted.

"That nit nurse isn't gonna get the better of the Menace," Dennis told Gnasher. "But they've done a pretty good job of locking the school this time!"

"GNASH!" growled Gnasher, scrabbling at the door of a storage cupboard.

Dennis frowned at him.

"Gnasher, what's got into you?" he demanded. "Menaces don't hide in cupboards! Pull yourself together! Are you a tripe hound or a mouse?"

Gnasher bared his teeth and gave a menacing growl.

"That's more like it!" Dennis declared. "Come on, there's no way I'm letting them get your super-menacing fleas!"

The headmaster's office was straight ahead. The headmaster himself had

gone in the opposite direction and his
room was usually locked, but Dennis
suddenly had a strong hunch. He
reached out and turned the handle –
and the door swung open!

"I knew it!" cried Dennis. "My
menacing radar never lets me down!
The headmaster's so busy locking all
the other doors and windows, he's
forgotten about his own office!"

Dennis and Gnasher dashed inside.

"Get sniffing, Gnasher!" Dennis

ordered. "Everybody knows the headmaster's got a secret escape route in here somewhere! It's our only chance!"

Gnasher worked his way around the edges of the room, sniffing for all he was worth, while Dennis looked behind picture frames, checked drawers in case they were secret passageways and pulled books out of the shelves in case they activated a secret panel.

They found plenty of things.

Gnasher found a half-eaten bun, dozens of empty sweet wrappers and about half a ton of dust.

Dennis found the headmaster's stash of catapults, his application to join the local knitting circle and his collection of witty but rude comments for the end-of-year reports, as well as an almost-unused case of stink bombs.

On any ordinary day Dennis would have been delighted with these discoveries, but right now all he needed was a way out.

"It's got to be in here somewhere!" he roared, thumping his fist down on the desk.

Suddenly there was a grinding noise and the desk slid aside to reveal a flight of steps leading down to a tunnel.

"We found it!" Dennis cheered.

Gnasher barked in excitement and together they raced down the narrow

steps. They were so happy that they completely forgot about keeping quiet.

Dennis was just following Gnasher into the thin tunnel when he felt a grip of steel around his ankle.

"Oh no you don't!" bellowed the headmaster. "It's the nit nurse for you, my lad!"

Dennis fought and struggled, but he was surrounded. Mr Pump took his legs while the headmaster grabbed his arms, and together they carried him back to the dreaded corridor. Gnasher ran alongside them, biting their ankles, but they were

18

wearing rubber ankle protectors.
They had thought of everything! The
other kids stared in horror as the
Menace was carried past them and
the door of the sick bay swung open.
The headmaster and Mr Pump flung
Dennis inside, threw Gnasher after
him and then slammed the door shut,
panting heavily.

"We've done it!" the headmaster
cried, beads of sweat rolling down
his forehead. "We've got him
at last!"

Inside the sick bay, Dennis turned around slowly. The nit nurse was standing facing him, her beefy arms folded across her chest and her warty face wearing a horrible smile of triumph. Dennis heard Gnasher give a low whine.

"Don't give her the satisfaction, Gnasher!" he hissed. "We're menaces, and she hasn't got us yet!"

"It's all over," said the nit nurse, taking a step forward.

"It's not over till the fat lady sings," said Dennis.

The nit nurse opened her mouth to reply but Dennis held up a hand.

"That wasn't an invitation to start singing," he added. "I don't want my eardrums to burst, thanks."

The nit nurse went bright red with fury.

"You'll regret that!" she snarled.

She flicked a switch and suddenly a machine in the corner started to hum ominously. There was a seat in the centre of it, and on the seat was the biggest mountain of food that Dennis had ever seen. Crisps, pies, sausages and sweets were bathed in a soft light, and wafts of a delicious smell floated under Dennis's nose.

Dennis let out a groan and took a step

towards the machine, his eyes swirling. Gnasher's eyes were closed as he drank in the wonderful smells.

"That's right," whispered the nit nurse in her softest voice. "Step closer. The food is all yours."

In one hand she held a nit comb, and in the other was a syringe, filled with the anti-stinky-cold jab.

"The – food – so – amazing – can't – resist –" Dennis stammered, moving still closer to the machine.

Outside, the remaining kids from the class huddled together as the headmaster rubbed his hands together and chuckled. They heard a yell and a cry, and then the door opened a crack.

"Headmaster," said the gravelly voice of the nit nurse. "Dennis has been overpowered! Come and see this historic moment!"

The headmaster rushed for the door as the classmates stared at each other in shock, and Walter the Softy fainted again.

The class waited outside and listened. There was absolute silence from inside the room. The kids exchanged looks of horror and disbelief. Was this really the end of the Menace?

Suddenly there was a loud, familiar cackle. The class rushed to the door and burst into the room. The nit nurse and the headmaster were both trapped inside the Dennis Device. Standing next to it, laughing, with his hands on his hips was . . .

DENNIS!

"No more nit inspections today!" he announced. "Now we're gonna have some flea inspections! Go for it, Gnasher!"

With a skilled scratch of his back paw, Gnasher sent two of his super-menacing fleas whizzing across the room. One landed on the nit nurse and one on the headmaster.

"Mummy!" wailed the headmaster.

"EEEK!" screeched the nit nurse. "I can't bear fleas! Get it off me!"

"Just think how they feel," Dennis chortled. "Fleas like that only live on menaces. Landing on you two could ruin their reputation!"

The class cheered as the headmaster struggled in vain to get free.

"There's no point trying to get out," said Dennis. "That thing was built to hold me – there's no way you could break out of it!"

"But Dennis, how did you resist all that food?" asked Curly, staring at the piles of grub that had been squashed when the headmaster sat down.

"They made one simple mistake," said Dennis. "They underestimated the Menace! It wasn't easy, but I knew I had to resist the temptation. I tricked the nit nurse into getting too close to the machine – and then

Gnasher shoved her in!"

"And then the headmaster got caught when he tried to pull her out?" Pie Face guessed. "This is the best Menace ever, Dennis!"

"I declare the rest of today a school holiday!" said Dennis.

There was another loud cheer from the rest of the class and then they all stampeded out towards the Beanotown sweet shop. Dennis paused at the door and looked back with a chuckle.

"Don't worry," he said. "Walter's out here and I'm sure he'll set you free . . . just as soon as you can stop him fainting at the sight of the nit nurse!"

DENNIS THE DENTIST

Dennis's parents had tried their best to ignore it.

Dad had polished all his golf clubs. Mum had washed all the net curtains. They had both watched a really boring documentary about spoons.

But it was no use.

"We have to face it," said Mum. "It's time for Dennis and Bea to go to the dentist."

Dad buried his head in his hands.

"What have I done to deserve this?" he groaned.

Mum stood up,

looking grim.

"Come on," she said. "The sooner we get it over with, the better."

Outside, Dennis was practising his skateboarding moves with Curly, while Pie Face tried to keep Bea under control.

"Dentist!" Bea hollered, bashing Pie Face over the head with her rattle.

"Bad luck, mate," said Curly.

"Last time I went to the dentist, he fainted," said Pie Face, rubbing his head.

"That was because of your stinky breath," said Curly.

"I like him, though," Pie Face went on. "He found a whole bit of pie that

I'd missed, stuck on one of my back teeth."

"Was that when he fainted?" asked Dennis with a grin.

He kick flicked his skateboard into his hands and Curly shook his head.

"I don't get it," he said. "Can't you think of a menace that'll get you out of the trip to the dentist?"

"Are you kidding?" said Dennis. "The dentist is brilliant – all that equipment gives me loads of ideas for menaces!"

"YOWEEEE!" yelled Pie Face, rocketing out of his seat.

He was clutching his finger – Bea had just bitten down on it.

"Sort your

sister out, Dennis!" he bawled.

"She's hungry," Dennis chuckled. "Anyway, you should know better by now than to put your finger near her mouth. That's another good thing about the dentist – he keeps our gnashers nice and strong, right Bea?"

"Gnash!" said Bea, baring her pearly white teeth.

"Gnash!" added Gnasher, champing his teeth together.

Mr Hickling, the Beanotown dentist, was a nervous man at the best of times. He was losing his hair because he tugged on it so much.

He jumped at loud noises. He had developed a tic that made his eyebrow jump up and down. It came on when he was especially worried about something. This morning, his eyebrow was moving so fast it was almost a blur.

"What a day!" he groaned to the receptionist, Kylie. "How could you do this to me?"

"I'm sorry, sir," said Kylie, who didn't look at all sorry. "You had lots of free appointments today. I didn't think it mattered who the patients were."

"Didn't think it mattered . . ." repeated Mr Hickling in a horrified whisper. "I've already had to treat Billy Whizz, Minnie and all the Bash Street Kids this morning. Look at the state of my treatment room!"

Kylie peered into the room and looked at the mess. Billy had raced around the room at top speed, until the dental nurse started to feel dizzy and had to lie down. Then he had shot into the seat so fast that he had melted the plastic cover.

Minnie had brought her water pistols with her, filled with week-old custard, and held them to Mr Hickling's head as he had checked her teeth. Then she had fired them both at the ceiling, which was now dripping with yellow goo.

The Bash Street Kids had insisted on all being treated at the same time, so they could write about it for their next school project. They had squeezed into the room until Mr Hickling could hardly move. The smell of stale school dinners and unwashed uniforms had filled the air.

Then Sydney had added fizzing powder to the coloured rinse, Toots had used the plaque-removing tablets to play tiddlywinks and Spotty had used the dental nurse's tweezers to burst a large zit on the tip of his nose. Mr Hickling had tried to take a plaster cast of Plug's teeth, but they were so large that they had broken all his moulds.

The dental nurse had collapsed in the corner.

"And now you tell me I have to see Dennis and Bea this afternoon," Mr Hickling continued. "I knew I should have taken the day off."

He rubbed his head and his eyebrow flickered up and down even faster than before.

"Never mind," said Kylie. "It's not all bad news. Your next patient is a very good boy indeed."

Mr Hickling peered into the waiting room and gave a sigh of relief.

Dennis, Bea and their parents arrived at the Beanotown Dental Surgery in plenty of time for their appointment. Mum and Dad took deep breaths and took out their list of orders. They had made a list of everything that they could imagine Dennis and Bea might do.

"Don't try to bite Mr Hickling's finger again, Bea," said Mum, ticking off the list. "No swinging from the mobile on the ceiling. No spitting competitions with the coloured rinse."

"No cleaning your catapult with the polishing brush," Dad continued, fixing Dennis with a beady eye. "No using the chair as an ejector seat."

Dennis grinned happily.

"That was a great menace," he remembered.

At that moment, Mr Hickling peered around the door. His eyebrow started to twitch again when he saw Dennis.

"D-Dennis," he said in a hoarse whisper.

"Hi, Mr Hickling!" said Dennis, jumping out of his chair.

"Best behaviour, remember?" hissed Dad. "Or there'll be no comics for a month!"

Dennis followed Mr Hickling out of the waiting room and Mum and Dad looked at each other.

"Last year it took five minutes before the dental nurse ran out screaming," said Dad.

"Don't remind me," Mum replied, groaning. "At least Dennis never docs the same menaces twice, and he actually likes Mr Hickling. How bad can it really get?"

Dad looked slightly relieved, but Bea just gave a gap-toothed grin.

In the treatment room, Dennis jumped into the chair and looked at the mess and the yellow goo with pleasure.

"I guess you've had Minnie here?" he enquired. "What new instruments have you got?"

Mr Hickling tried to stop his knees knocking together.

"N-no n-new ones this year, D-Dennis," he said. "Er . . . open wide."

Dennis opened his mouth and Mr Hickling wiped his sweaty forehead.

Ten minutes later, Mr Hickling's eyebrow was moving more slowly.

"Very good, Dennis," he said. "Nice strong gnashers."

Mr Hickling turned away to check on the nurse, who was just starting to come round. Dennis spotted a small box on the side with a large label on it:

OLD DENTAL EQUIPMENT TO BE THROWN AWAY

"What a waste," said Dennis under his breath. "I'll help Mr Hickling out and get rid of these for him."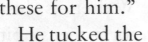

He tucked the box into his pocket and strolled out to the waiting room.

"Your turn," he told Bea.

Mum and Dad looked at him in astonishment.

"Has Mr Hickling fainted?" asked Mum.

"Nope," Dennis replied with a wide grin. "No menaces. He's fine."

Mum and Dad should have been suspicious. They had known Dennis long enough, after all. But they were tired after worrying all night, and they still had to take Bea in there. So they just smiled at Dennis and hurried into the treatment room with Bea.

Suddenly the telephone rang and Kylie answered it.

"Hello, Mr Hickling's surgery, can I help you?" she said. "Oh yes, Madam. Dear little Walter is just upstairs, Madam. He got a teensy bit scared when the chair rose up and he just needed a little lie down."

Dennis smiled.

When Kylie put down the telephone and looked up, she was surprised to see that Dennis had completely disappeared.

Dennis raced up a narrow flight of stairs and found a door at the top with a sign on it:

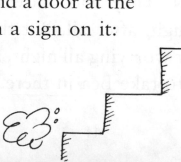

SHHHH!

FLUFFY ROOM

FOR SPECIAL SOFTIES.

WALK ON TIPPY-TOES PLEASE.

STRICTLY NO MENACING!

Dennis pulled the little box out of his pocket and found a scraper inside. A menacing grin spread over his face.

"Only softies are scared of the dentist," he said to himself. "Someone needs to help Walter get over his fear!"

Dennis turned the handle and the door opened with a loud creeeaaak.

He peered inside and paused in horror. The dentist's chair in the corner was pink and made of puffed satin. The walls were painted with pictures of chicks and bunnies, and tinkling fairy music was playing in the background. The smell of roses filled the air.

"Yuck," said Dennis. "I never knew Mr Hickling had a torture room!"

Walter the Softy was lying on a bed, fast asleep. He was wearing a badge that read 'I've been a good boy for the dentist'.

Dennis bent down beside Walter.

"Open wide," he said. "I'm Dennis the dentist, and there's nothing to be scared of. I'm just gonna menace all the bad teeth right out of your mouth!"

Walter's eyes flickered and his mouth twitched.

"Now just lie very still," said Dennis,

leaning forward.

At that moment, Walter opened his eyes. He saw Dennis standing over him clutching a scraper and wearing his most menacing expression.

"HEEELLLPPP!" Walter squealed, leaping to his feet.

"Don't panic, said Dennis. "The dentist is really busy, so I thought I'd help him out and finish the job off, that's all!"

"Get away from me, you hairy, hulking, horrible menace!" cried Walter. "Mr Hickling said we can wait for my tooth to come out by itself because I'm so sensitive to the sight of blood!"

"Aha, so you do have a tooth that's ready to come out!" cried Dennis. "Nothing to be scared of, you silly softy – just one little tug and it's all over!"

Dennis selected a pair of tooth pliers from his little box and Walter backed up against the dentist's chair in the corner of the room.

"Geronimo!" yelled Dennis, charging at Walter with his head down.

Walter flew backwards into the chair and the chair skidded back, hitting an old-fashioned piece of equipment labelled 'Laughing Gas'. The switch turned from 'Off' to 'On' and a mask fell down and covered Walter's mouth and nose. Then there was a hissing noise and the mask filled with a faint mist.

Walter relaxed and started to giggle.

"It's the Menace!" he chuckled.

"Huh?" said Dennis, pausing.

"He's going to do a menace on me!" hooted Walter, tears of laughter running down his face. "I'm doomed! Hee hee hee! Ho ho ho! Ha ha ha!"

"The softy's gone loopy!" said Dennis, eyeing the laughing gas machine. "Pity it's too heavy to carry with me! What a brilliant bit of menacing equipment that would be!"

Suddenly something small and white popped out of Walter's mouth and landed in his hand.

He had laughed so hard that his wobbly tooth had fallen out!

"Hee hee hee!" giggled Walter. "My tooth has come out! You know what that means, Menace?"

"Yep," said Dennis, folding his arms and frowning. "It means that you have a brilliant tool for menacing the girls – they hate teeth!"

"No," said Walter, wiping his streaming eyes. "It means that the tooth fairy will be visiting me tonight, and leaving me a lovely present!"

"Tooth fairy?" repeated Dennis. "Yuck! I'm getting out of here!"

He hurtled out of the room and raced downstairs, just as his parents walked out of the treatment room with Bea.

"There you are, Dennis," said Mum. "Time to go. You've both been very well behaved – you can have extra pocket money for a month!"

They walked out into Beanotown High Street and Dad dipped his hand into his pocket.

"Here's some money for sweets," he told Dennis. "Take Bea and go and buy yourselves some treats for being so good."

Mum and Dad walked off, shaking their heads in amazement. Dennis grabbed Bea and raced into the sweet shop. There were sweets of every shape and colour. There were fizzy sweets and chewy sweets, sweets that exploded in your mouth and sweets that made steam come out of your ears. Dennis and Bea filled a paper bag with all of their favourites. Then suddenly Dennis spotted something that gave him a brilliant idea. Tucked away in a far corner was a jar of sweets that were shaped exactly like teeth.

"Bea, we're gonna play at being fairies,"
said Dennis with a menacing chuckle.

Bea looked at her big brother in
amazement, but he just winked at her.

Two hours later, Bea and Dennis were underneath Walter the Softy's bedroom window. Dennis took out his packet of Mr Hickling's extra-strong, extra-long dental floss. He tied one end around Bea's waist and threw the other end over the branch of a nearby tree.

"You know what to do?" he whispered.

Bea nodded and Dennis pulled on the dental floss. Bea shot up until she was dangling right outside Walter's window. She balanced on the windowsill and quietly inched open the window. Then she crept inside. Walter was fast asleep, his eyes covered with a pink

satin eye mask. He was wearing duck-egg-blue fluffy earmuffs to keep out loud noises. Bea chuckled and slipped her hand under his pillow. Just as Dennis had said, there was Walter's tooth, waiting for the tooth fairy. Bea took the tooth and stuffed handfuls of teeth sweets in its place. Then she took Dennis's bottle of squirty fake blood out of her pocket. She pushed the nozzle under Walter's pillow and squeezed.

Suddenly Walter gave a loud snore! Bea froze, but Walter didn't wake up. She put the bottle back into her pocket, hopped up on to the windowsill and waved at Dennis. He lowered her down and she handed him Walter's tooth.

"Excellent," he said, stuffing it into his pocket. "This'll get the girls screaming their heads off. Good job, Bea."

They stared up at Walter's window and then grinned at each other.

"Poor old Walter, being so scared of teeth and blood and the dentist," said Dennis, shaking his head. "Well, if that's doesn't cure him of his fears, nothing will!"

Next morning, Walter yawned and stretched. He took off his pink satin eye mask and his duck-egg-blue earmuffs, and sat up to wait for his mumsy to bring him breakfast in bed. Then he clapped his hands together as he remembered his tooth.

"Oh, I wonder what the tooth fairy has brought me!" he simpered, lifting his pillow.

"AAARRRRGGGHHH!"

The high-pitched scream echoed around Beanotown. Cats dived for cover, their paws over their ears. Dogs ran towards Walter's house in a frenzied pack. Windows shattered and glass vases smashed. And in his sleep, a boy in black-and-red-striped pyjamas gave a wide, menacing smile.

HELPING HANDS

Everyone in Dennis's street was fed up with the racket.

"I hate hospitals!" came the holler from Dennis's house. "I'm in agony! I've had enough!"

"We've all had enough!" roared the Colonel. "Shut up, Dennis!"

Then the Colonel got the shock of his life. Dennis was skateboarding

towards him down the street!

"But . . . but . . . if you're out here . . . who's making all that noise?" the Colonel stammered.

Dennis rolled his eyes.

"It's Dad," he said. "He had to go into hospital this morning to have an ingrowing toenail removed."

"An ingrowing toenail?" blustered the Colonel. "Great Scott, that's nothing! My men face death in battle every day!"

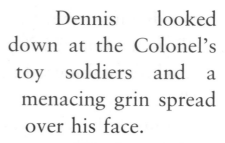

Dennis looked down at the Colonel's toy soldiers and a menacing grin spread over his face.

"Yeah, there are some pretty dangerous-looking worms lurking in your garden, Colonel," he said with a chuckle.

"No more cheek from you, young man, or I'll have you court-martialled!" bellowed the Colonel.

Another earth-shattering groan emerged from Dennis's house and the Colonel's face grew even redder.

"Take your war wounds like a soldier, man!" he trumpeted up at Dennis's parents' bedroom window. "Show a little style!"

Dennis skateboarded over the Colonel's toes, shot up his garden path and crashed in through the back door. Mum was cooking lunch, with swathes of cotton wool sticking out of her ears. Bea was sitting in her highchair with a saucepan over her head to block out the sound of Dad moaning.

"What's for lunch?" asked Dennis.

"About half past one," said Mum.

"I said WHAT'S FOR LUNCH?" Dennis bawled.

"Oh, underneath the stairs behind Bea's headless dolls," Mum replied.

"Never mind," groaned Dennis.

He skidded into the hall and saw a familiar black tail sticking out of the umbrella stand. Even Gnasher was trying to block out the sounds from upstairs. Dennis sped up to his parents' bedroom and stood in the doorway with his arms folded.

"Dad, you've got the whole street complaining," he said. "It's brilliant! Even I've never managed that!"

"I'm not trying to be a menace,

60

you menace!" Dad roared. "I'm in agony! I may not survive!"

"I reckon most people pull through after a toenail operation," said Dennis, jumping on the bed with a grin.

"YOWEEE!" cried Dad as his foot bounced up and down.

"What was the operation like?" Dennis enquired. "Was there loads of blood? Did they pull out the nail without any anaesthetic?"

He pulled out his menace notebook and pencil, and got ready to take notes.

"Heartless boy," said Dad, sinking

back against his pillow. "Those doctors are animals! They're all just overgrown menaces getting paid to cause mischief! I won't be able to play golf for a week!"

"Shame," said Dennis. "Hmmm. . . overgrown menaces, eh?"

He leapt off the bed, raced out of the bedroom and slid down the banister, landing next to the umbrella stand. Dennis bent over and spoke to the quivering black tail of his favourite tripe hound.

"Gnasher, guess what," he said. "I'm considering a career in medicine."

On Monday morning, all across Beanotown, children were trudging to school, teachers were counting how many days were left until the next holiday, and Beanotown School was bracing itself for another week of mayhem.

"Minnie, don't do that," bellowed their form teacher during morning registration. "Pie Face, take your hand out of there immediately! Curly, stop that racket and put the drum kit away! Who put this whoopee cushion in my sandwich?"

"I think it was Walter, sir," said Dennis, aiming a paper plane at Bertie Blenkinsop's bottom.

"Sir, sir, it's not true sir!" Walter wailed.

"YOWCH!" squealed Bertie, leaping into the air and clutching his bottom.

"QUIET!" bawled the headmaster, who had just walked in.

Everyone sat down and a stray elastic band pinged the end of the headmaster's nose. He decided to ignore it.

"I have a very important task for you all," he announced. "I think it is very important for you all to feel that you are part of the Beanotown community . . ."

"I don't like the sound of this," Dennis whispered in Curly's ear.

". . . so I have decided that you

are all going to do something to help Beanotown," the headmaster continued.

"Sir, maybe Pie Face could help the butchers get rid of all their out-of-date pies," said Dennis.

"Walter could help clean out the sewers!" Curly suggested, snorting with laughter.

"Sir, I think Dennis should help in the beauty salon," shouted Minnie.

"I reckon you need it more than I do!" Dennis chortled.

"Silence!" the headmaster roared as he pulled a piece of paper out of his pocket. "I have drawn up a list of the possibilities and each of you must choose one."

The headmaster began to read out the options. Walter volunteered to spend a day in the Beanotown library. Bertie jumped at the chance to wash poodles at the Beanotown Dog Grooming Parlour. Dennis, Curly and Pie Face looked at each other in horror as the list went on.

"Washing cars at the garage?" continued the headmaster. "Thank you, Billy, I'm sure you'll make fast work of that. Working in the fashion section of the Beanotown charity shop? . . . ah, is that your hand I see, Minnie?"

"No!" growled Minnie.

"Excellent, excellent, I'm sure

you'll enjoy yourself. Now, let me see, a pair of helping hands wanted at Beanotown Hospital."

Dennis's hand shot into the air. The whole class stared at him in amazement.

"What on earth are you doing, mate?" hissed Curly.

"Are you . . . are you . . . actually volunteering, Dennis?" enquired the headmaster, taking off his glasses and wiping them on his tie.

"He's gone crazy," said Pie Face.

"Yes sir, I'll do that one," said Dennis with a wide grin.

He rubbed his hands together in glee as the headmaster wrote down his name.

"Don't worry, I haven't gone loopy," Dennis told his best friends in a whisper. "I'm just gonna pick up some top menacing tips. Dad says that the Beanotown doctors are the biggest menaces he's ever met!"

When Dennis arrived at Beanotown Hospital, a nurse met him at the door.

"I'm Nurse Venom," she said in a snooty voice. "And who might you be?"

"I'm your helping hands for the day," said Dennis, with a grin.

Nurse Venom looked at Dennis and then she looked at Gnasher. Her nose wrinkled up in disgust.

"What is that?" she enquired, pointing at Gnasher.

"A tripe hound," said Dennis. "Did you know that it's rude to point?"

"This is a hospital, not a rubbish tip," said the nurse. "That tripe hound is the most unhygienic creature I have ever seen – or smelt!"

Gnasher wagged his tail and Dennis gave Nurse Venom a wide smile.

"Thanks," he said. "We've put in a lot of hard work."

"Well it's not

coming in here!" said Nurse
Venom. "Tie him up outside."

"But menacing dogs aren't
meant to be hygienic!" said
Dennis. "Besides, he doesn't
have a lead."

The nurse's eyes narrowed.

"We'll see about that," she said,
pulling a rope from a hook on the
wall. "Tie him up out here, or you're
not coming in."

Dennis scowled and turned to
Gnasher.

"I'm really sorry," he whispered.
"But just think about all the great
menaces I'll pick up here! I'll get you
two strings of sausages to make it up
to you."

Dennis left a furious Gnasher tied
to the hospital railings and followed
Nurse Venom into the hospital.

"Put these on," said Nurse Venom,

handing
Dennis a pair
of peach-coloured
overalls.

"No way!" said Dennis, appalled.

Nurse Venom narrowed her eyes to slits and bent down until her puffy face was inches away from Dennis.

"Wear them or clear off," she snapped.

Thinking of all the menacing tips he hoped to pick up, Dennis bit his tongue and pulled on the disgusting overalls.

"Now, your first job is to take breakfast round to all the elderly patients on Snot Ward," said Nurse Venom. "I'll be right behind you."

Dennis pushed the breakfast trolley along. It was piled high with plates of congealed eggs and cold baked beans. He plonked the first plate down in front of an old man.

"Take it away!" shouted the old man. "I don't want that muck!"

"EAT IT UP!" bellowed Nurse Venom.

Dennis put another plate down in front of the next patient, an old lady with her leg in plaster.

"I'm not eating that!" she squawked.

"You'll eat it and like it!" roared Nurse Venom.

None of the patients wanted breakfast, but they didn't have any choice. Nurse Venom shouted and bellowed at them until they started to eat the horrible food.

"When do I get to help out the doctors?" Dennis asked Nurse Venom when all the breakfasts had been delivered.

"Help the doctors?" repeated Nurse Venom with a cold laugh. "You're not going anywhere near the doctors! I want you here on my ward all day, helping me!"

She turned on her heel and marched

back to her desk, but Dennis stayed where he was, frowning. Then a twinkle came into his eyes, and a smile played around his mouth.

Dennis hurried over to the nearest patient.

"I'm collecting for the breakfast fund," he said, leaning over and whispering his plan into the man's ear.

A toothy grin spread over the man's face.

"That's the best idea I've heard since I came in here," he said, pressing a coin into Dennis's hand.

The word spread fast through the ward and soon Dennis had a pocketful of coins. He pulled off the peach-coloured overalls and raced out of the hospital and across the road to a snack van that had just arrived. Within minutes he was back in the ward with armfuls of hot bacon sandwiches, crisps, chocolate bars, chips, hamburgers and hot dogs. Soon the patients of Snot Ward were wolfing their new breakfasts down as fast as they could. The only sounds were gulps and satisfied sighs.

"WHAT do you think you're doing?" shrieked a voice in Dennis's ear.

Nurse Venom was purple with rage.

"Leave the boy alone!" shouted the patients. "He can come again! We like him!"

"Leave my ward at once!" said the nurse. "These patients aren't here to enjoy themselves!"

"Shall I go and help the doctors?" said Dennis.

"Certainly not!" said Nurse Venom. "You can go up to the maternity ward! All the babies will be asleep, so you can't cause any mischief up there!"

"Wanna bet?" grumbled Dennis under his breath.

He shoved his hands into his

pockets and trudged along the hospital corridors towards the maternity ward. But just before he reached it, he spotted the doctors' staff room. There were several doctors inside, but what caught Dennis's eye was the spare white doctor's coat that was hanging up on a hook.

"If only I could think of a way to get past all those doctors," he said under his breath.

There was no menacing gear around, so Dennis slipped into the maternity ward – and clamped his hands over his ears. It sounded as if every single baby on the ward was yelling at the top of its lungs. It was almost as deafening as Bea's crying. Dennis spotted a group of nurses and skidded towards them, bursting in on their conversation.

". . . and the pastel yellow handbag

didn't match my – who are you?"
snapped one of the nurses.

"Nurse Venom sent me up to help
you out," said Dennis. "But if you
want me to talk about pastel yellow
handbags, you'll have a long wait."

"No cheek from you, young man!"
said the nurse,

going
bright red.
"I've got just the job for
you! All the babies need to have
their nappies changed. Chop chop!"

A menacing grin spread over Dennis's
face as he grabbed a pile of nappies
and headed for the babies. He had
changed tons of Bea's nappies, and he
knew that if he could deal with them,
he could deal with anything. Besides,

he would ten times rather be changing
nappies than talking about
handbags.

Before the babies knew what was
happening, they were cleaned and
changed, and their dirty nappies
were in a basket in the middle of
the room.

"Now, my little menaces-in-the-making," said Dennis, rubbing his hands together. "The lesson of the day is that you can find menacing weapons anywhere."

Dennis grabbed a broom and hung the nappy basket on the end of it. The stench was incredible, but it didn't bother the Menace.

"When you've smelt Bea's nappies, these are nothing," he told the babies.

Dennis crept past the nurses, who were discussing nail polish colours, out of the maternity ward and back to the open door of the doctors' staff room. Then he stuck the basket into the staff room on the end of the pole. Dennis counted to three, and then he heard several loud thumps as the doctors hit the floor.

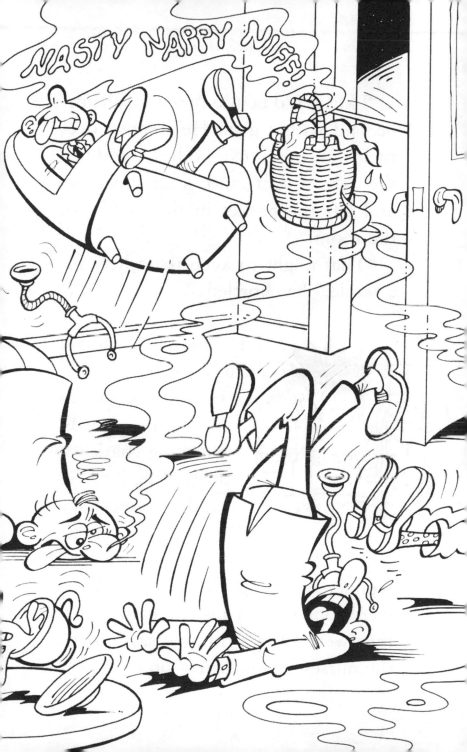

"I knew it'd be too much for them," he said with a grin. He stepped over their unconscious bodies, grabbed the white coat and a stethoscope, and left the basket in the middle of the room.

"That ought to keep them here for a while," he chortled.

Dennis had a brilliant afternoon.

He did the rounds of all the wards, checking patients, diagnosing illnesses and prescribing medicine. The nurses were a bit puzzled and wondered where the usual doctors were, but Dennis just explained that they were all in a training session and the nurses let him carry on.

Dennis was just writing out a prescription for a softy on Fairyland Ward (three spoonfuls of cod liver oil twenty times a day) when he spotted Nurse Venom. She didn't recognise him in his disguise.

"Oh doctor," she simpered. "Is there anything I can do to help?"

"Hmmm," said Dennis, rubbing his chin thoughtfully. "Don't we have someone from Beanotown School here to help us out? Where is he?"

"Oh, he's a terrible menace," said Nurse Venom with a yellow-toothed smile. "My nephew Walter told me all about him, but he's not getting away with his menacing on my ward! I'm much too smart for him!"

"Excellent, nurse," said Dennis. "Now, if you could just empty all the bedpans on this ward?"

Nurse Venom's face fell.

"Empty . . . bedpans?" she repeated.

"At once, nurse!" Dennis roared.

Nurse Venom jumped and scurried off to do as she was told. Dennis chuckled and was about to leave the ward when the doors burst open and all the doctors rushed in, still staggering from the effects of the nappies.

"Time to scarper!" said Dennis, throwing off the white coat.

Before anyone could stop him, Dennis was out of Fairyland Ward and hammering down the stairs to the exit. But as he skidded past Snot Ward, the elderly patients called out to him.

"We need your help!" said one old man. "You cheered up breakfast this morning. Reckon you can cheer up our dreary hospital radio?"

A grin spread over Dennis's face.

"I'll see what I can do," he said with a wink.

Dennis popped his head around the radio booth and told the DJ that Nurse Venom had been calling him names. The furious DJ raced off to give her a piece of his mind.

Dennis zoomed into the booth, opened the CD player and grimaced

when he saw the name of the CD
– '101 Cheesy Songs You've Heard
Before'.

"That's not gonna make the patients
get better," said Dennis, flinging the
CD out of the window (and knocking
Sergeant Slipper's hat off).

Beanotown Hospital had never known a day like it. Dennis played the loudest, hottest music he could lay his hands on.

"Music is the best medicine, folks!" he roared into the microphone. "Get out of your beds and dance around the wards! If you can't get out of bed, just chuck your bedpans around! Nurse Venom'll clean it up!"

The whole hospital was rocking as the elderly patients bounced up and down on their mattresses, played drums with their bedpans and gave each other rides up and down the wards on operation trolleys. The doctors and nurses flew around the hospital in a panic, with no idea how to stop the mayhem.

"We've lost control!" shrieked Nurse Venom. "Call the army!"

"That's enough out of you!" said an elderly man, flinging his blanket over the nurse and shoving her into a laundry basket.

Dennis peered out of the booth and grinned.

"Elderly menacing," he said. "Excellent."

He slipped through the crowds of dancing patients and panicking doctors, and collected Gnasher from the railings outside.

"I don't think I'm gonna be a doctor after all," said Dennis as they headed towards the butcher's shop. "I don't think that the medical world is ready for me yet!"

Collect all ten titles . . .

ISBN: 978-1-84539-095-2

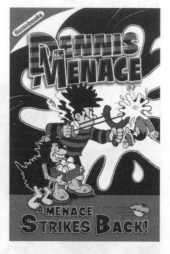

ISBN: 978-1-84539-096-9

ISBN: 978-1-84539-204-8

ISBN: 978-1-84539-213-0

...to complete the menacing series

ISBN: 978-1-84539-098-3

ISBN: 978-1-84539-097-6

ISBN: 978-1-84539-205-5

ISBN: 978-1-84539-214-7

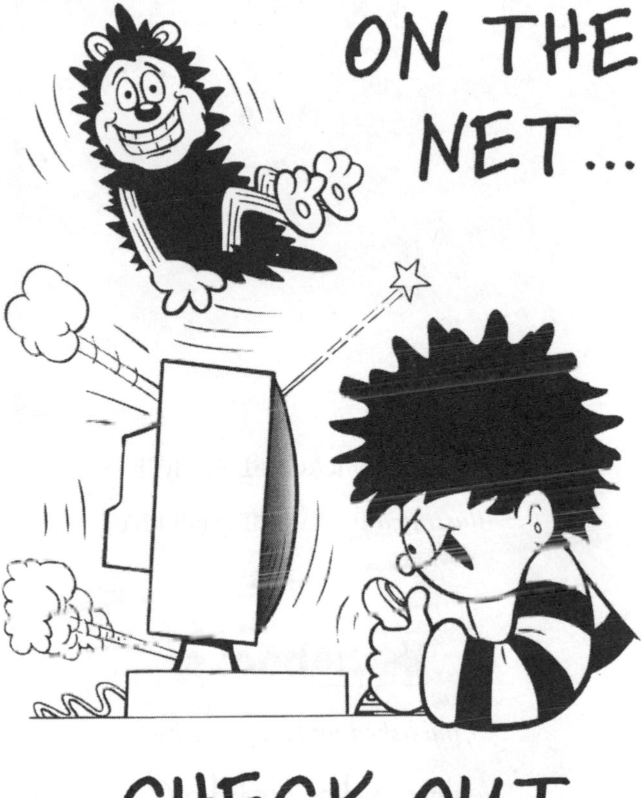

Written by RACHEL ELLIOT

Illustrated by BARRIE APPLEBY

published under licence by

CHILDREN'S BOOKS

185 Fleet Street, London, EC4A 2HS

10 9 8 7 6 5 4 3 2